Sesame Street babies™

Words/Palabras

airplane  avión

Illustrated by Peter Panas

This educational book was created in cooperation with Children's Television Workshop, producers of Sesame Street. Children do not have to watch the television show to benefit from this book. Workshop revenues from this product will be used to help support CTW projects.

shoe

zapato

comb

kite

cometa

sun

coat

fork

tenedor

cat

tree

árbol

bird

pájaro

dog

perro

telephone

teléfono

cake

house

casa

moon

luna

chair

table

mesa

rain

lluvia

_____   _____

butterfly

mariposa

ball

pants

pantalones

door

puerta

knife

cuchillo

bed

cama

umbrella
paraguas

fish

book

libro

shirt

camisa

car

automóvil

plate

bicycle

bicicleta

bread

hat

sombrero

three

4 four

seven

8 eight

ocho

nine

10 ten   diez